PENNY PICKS
THE PERFECT PET

Written by Carol Szuminsky
Illustrated by Jenny Prest

Peanut Butter Press

CONTENTS

PENNY PICKS THE PERFECT PET PENNY PICKS TH
RFECT PET PENNY PICKS THE PERFECT PET PENN

Chapter One: Please! Please! Please!

Penny woke up to the sound of birds singing in the tree outside her window. As she lay in bed, she thought the same thoughts she thought every morning.

"There's one thing I want more than anything else in the whole world! I would like a pet of my own to take care of and love. My three best friends all have pets, and I'm really good at feeding and playing with their animals. I know I'm big enough," she told herself.

Then Penny whispered to the little bird on the closest branch, "Maybe today will be the day my parents will finally realize that I'm ready to have a pet."

Penny bounced out of bed and got dressed quickly. She hurried downstairs to her favourite breakfast of pancakes with maple syrup. Instead of butter, she liked to spread a little peanut butter on top. Then she would pour on the syrup and watch it flow, like a river of liquid gold.

As she ate her pancakes, Penny was still trying to decide which kind of pet she liked the most.

$\mathcal{J}$ust then, the doorbell rang. Penny rushed to see who was at the door. It was Jamie, her very best friend.

"Hi, Penny!" greeted Jamie. "Would you like to help me walk Quincy and Gus?"

"You bet I would!" exclaimed Penny. "I'll go ask my mom."

Penny's mother knew how much her daughter loved Quincy and Gus. She was pleased to see Penny taking some responsibility for Jamie's dogs.

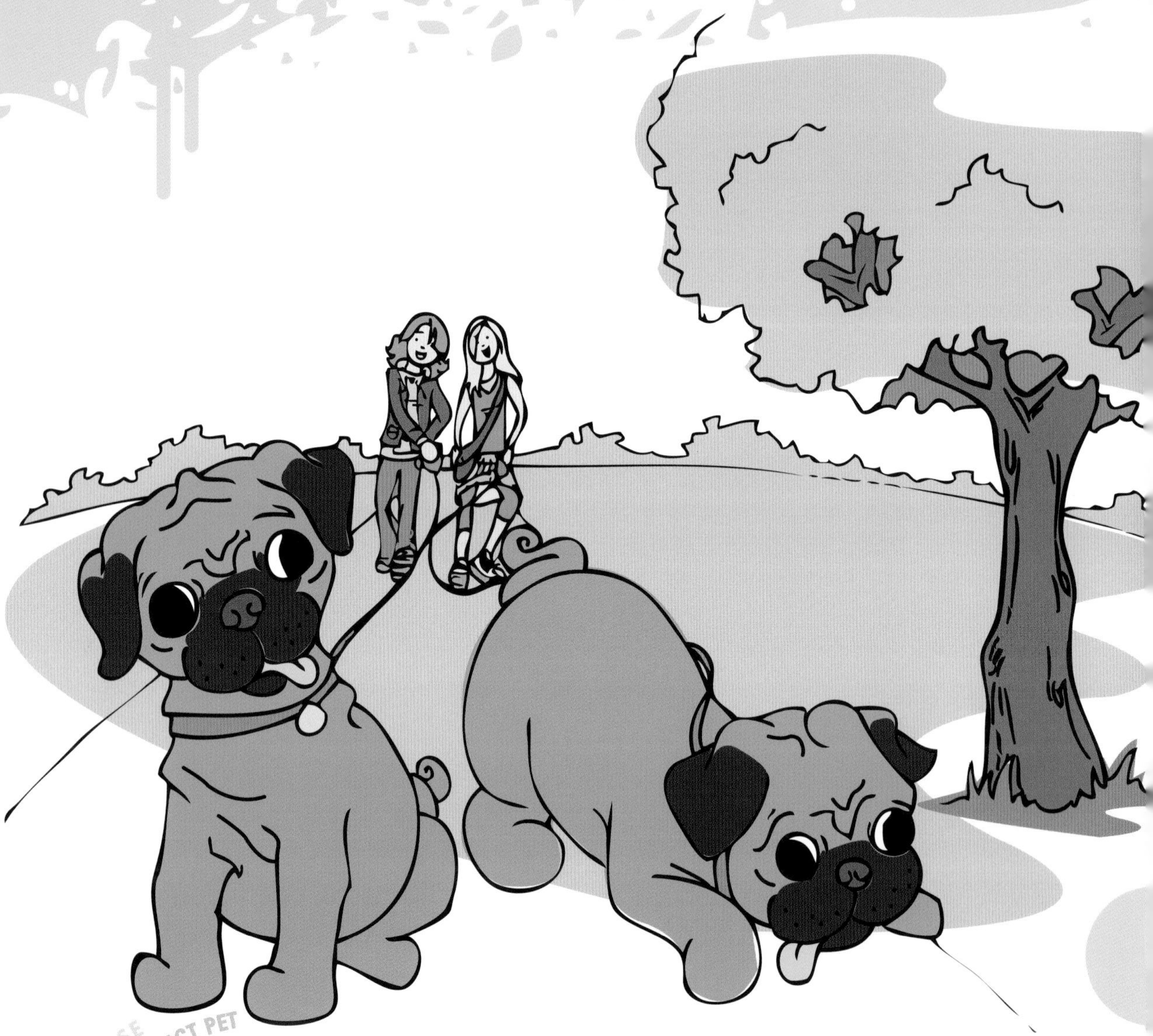

Quincy and Gus were pugs and quite pudgy. On their walks, they waddled along, panting. All that walking made the pugs hot and tired. As soon as they got back to Jamie's house, they would wriggle around in the thick grass to cool off.

Penny had so much fun playing with Quincy and Gus. The dogs always gave her wet kisses all over her face. They liked it when Penny used their squeaky toys to play fetch with them.

"Boy, Quincy and Gus are sure getting their exercise today!" laughed Penny.

She knew that it was important for the dogs to run and play so they would stay healthy and happy. Jamie's mother had told her that the dogs had feelings and their own personalities, just like people. Quincy was always ready for an adventure. Gus, on the other hand, was a bit shy and would wait for Quincy to check things out. Both dogs were friendly and gentle. Penny especially loved the funny expressions on their cute, wrinkled faces. She wondered whether a dog would be the best choice for a pet.

On the way back from Jamie's house, Penny dropped in to visit Justin, another favourite friend. Justin had two pet rats that were very smart and loving. Ralph and Roger would watch quietly while Justin worked on his homework. Doing schoolwork was more fun with a furry friend sitting on his shoulder. Sometimes Roger would take a little nibble out of one of the pages, but he would never eat the whole thing. Roger must have known that telling the teacher his rat ate his homework would not help Justin in school one bit.

When Penny got there, Justin was just giving Roger a slice of apple.

"Should I feed Ralph?" Penny asked.

"He's already finished eating his breakfast, but you can see whether he wants a few seeds for a treat," answered Justin.

Penny showed Ralph the food, and he ate it right out of her hand. She liked the way his little, pink tongue tickled when he licked her hand clean. Justin loved Ralph and Roger, but Penny wasn't sure that a rat would be the right pet for her family. She had to give this decision more thought.

mily was Penny's other best friend. She had a hamster she called Snowball because his fur was white and his body was roly-poly, just like a ball. Whenever Penny came over to play, the girls would spread out an old quilt on the floor and then make it all lumpy. After that, they would take Snowball out of his cage and watch him climb over the humps and bumps. Penny liked to cradle the fluffy, little creature against her body and pet his fur. She didn't even mind cleaning out his messy cage. She was certain that she would enjoy having a hamster to care for and love.

*L*ater that day, Penny's mother had a surprise for her.

"Penny, hop in the car. We're going for a ride," said her mom.

"Where are we going?" Penny asked curiously.

"Just wait and see," replied her mother.

In no time at all, they turned onto the road that led to Penny's favourite place to shop.

"Oh, I know! We're going to the mall! Will we have time to visit the pet store?" Penny asked eagerly.

"Yes. After we're finished our shopping, we'll go see the animals," her mother promised.

When Penny went to the mall with her parents, they usually let her spend a few minutes looking around the pet store. She really believed that one day her wish would come true, and she wanted to be ready to choose wisely when that time came.

Penny knew that she needed to think carefully about all the possible choices for a pet. She tried to visit different kinds of animals on every shopping trip, but somehow the hamsters always caught her eye. She often had a puppy in her arms when it was time to leave.

As Penny followed her mom around the mall, she stayed calm on the outside. Inside, she was secretly hoping that today might be the day that would hear those magic words... "Penny, you may pick your pet."

How could she pick a pet? She still hadn't decided which kind of animal she would like best. She sang softly to herself, "I wonder what would be — the perfect pet for me."

Her excitement bubbled over when they entered the pet store! There were soft, cuddly mammals that you could hold and pet, birds that looked and sounded so pretty, fish of all colours, shapes, and sizes, and interesting creatures like ferrets and prickly hedgehogs. Penny walked quickly past the stinging scorpions and hairy tarantula spiders.

"Mom, which kind of pet do you think would be best for me... and our family?" Penny questioned.

"Well, dear, remember that there's more to having a pet than just loving it. Taking care of an animal can be a lot of work. You must be careful to pick a pet that you know you will enjoy spending time with and never get tired of," answered her mother.

"I think I understand, Mom," replied Penny, "but it's so hard to decide which kind of pet that would be."

"You need to just be patient. Often the answer comes when you least expect it. You will know which kind of animal is best when the time is right," Penny's mom assured her, "but first your father and I need to be convinced that you are old enough and responsible enough to look after a pet."

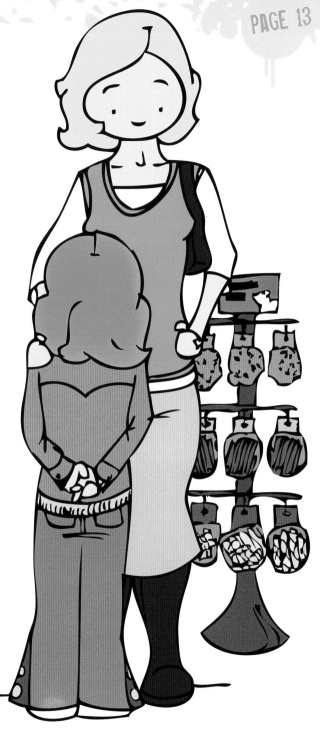

Her parents didn't really mind helping, but they wanted to be sure their daughter would do her share. They waited and watched for signs that Penny was ready to take on the responsibility of caring for an animal.

Days and weeks went by, and Penny was beginning to think she would never get a pet — not even a pretty goldfish she could watch swim around in its bowl. She was considering getting out her bug box and finding a fuzzy caterpillar.

PENNY PICKS THE PERFECT PET

PLEASE PLEASE PLEASE PLEASE

Chapter Two: The Purr-fect Opportunity

One afternoon, Penny was helping her mom pull weeds from their flower garden. Mrs. French, the neighbour from across the street, came over with her family's new kitten. They had named their kitten Marmalade because its fur was orange — just like the tasty marmalade jelly Penny ate with her peanut butter on toast.

"Penny, I was hoping that you would be able to take care of Marmalade for a week while our family goes camping," Mrs. French said kindly.

"Oh, Mom, may I? Please! Please! Please!" Penny pleaded.

Penny's mother answered with a "yes." She had decided that this would be the perfect opportunity for her daughter to show that she was really ready to have a pet.

"May I please hold Marmalade?" Penny asked politely.

"Of course, you may," replied Mrs. French, as she carefully placed Marmalade into Penny's arms.

Mrs. French was surprised to hear that Penny already knew that giving cats milk to drink could make them sick. Penny had learned this when a volunteer from an animal shelter spoke to her class about being a responsible pet owner.

Penny was so excited! Taking care of Marmalade would be just like having a pet of her very own. They went over to Mrs. French's house so Penny and her mom could find out everything they needed to know about taking care of the kitten. Mrs. French even showed them how to change the litter in Marmalade's litter box. That was when Penny realized that there was at least one thing about having a cat that was not fun.

Penny had to wait five whole days before she had the sweet, little kitten all to herself!

$\mathcal{M}$armalade was always doing things that made Penny laugh. It was fun to watch the little kitten play with a ball of wool or her catnip mouse. Penny would pick the kitten up ever so gently and whisper in her ear, "You're just so cute." Marmalade also liked paper bags. Sometimes she would crawl in and stay very still as if she was playing hide-and-seek. Other times, she would pounce on the bag or move around inside and make lots of noise. Penny guessed that Marmalade liked the crinkly sound the paper made.

The week passed, and every day Penny remembered to feed Marmalade and make time to play with the kitten. Her parents were impressed with her responsible behaviour, especially when she cleaned the litter box all by herself. They decided that she was now old enough to take care of a pet. The night the kitten went home, Penny was told the good news.

"Am I allowed to choose any kind of pet I want?" Penny asked her parents politely.

Her father answered. "Well, I've noticed that you seem to like animals that you can hold and that will snuggle up to you, so you probably wouldn't want to choose fish or something like a turtle or python," he suggested seriously. "On second thought, that kind of snake might want to snuggle around you!" he added with a tease in his voice.

Her mother didn't answer right away. She was thinking back to when she was a child. Then she spoke. "When I was growing up, I enjoyed all my pets. My family had a black dog with curly fur, two little hamsters, and a really big guinea pig," she said with a smile.

Penny giggled. "That might explain why I like puppies and hamsters so much," she told her mom.

Penny still wasn't sure which kind of animal she wanted most. She needed to spend more time gathering information before finally making her decision.

Penny knew the next day was Saturday. She asked if they could get up early and go to the pet store before it got too busy.

"Then I could look around really well and ask questions. I want to find out as much as I can about all the possible kinds of pets before I make my choice!" she stated. "I'll even take along a pencil and the shiny notepad that Auntie Barb gave me for my birthday."

Her parents agreed. She got into her pyjamas, brushed her teeth, and went right to bed. That night, Penny could hardly sleep. All she could think about was that she would soon have her very own pet!

Chapter Three: The Pet Store

The next morning, Penny was up bright and early. Quick as a bunny, she was all ready to go to the mall. She had decided that she would do some exploring on her own first so she would know the best questions to ask.

When Penny and her parents arrived at the pet store, she went straight to the rows of glass cases that held the unusual animals. There were rainbow skinks, crested and leopard geckos, bearded dragon lizards, and four different kinds of snakes. As Penny studied the interesting creatures in the terrariums, she began to imagine these animals in their tropical rainforest home. Instead of the glass terrarium, Penny could see the rather large panther chameleon sitting in the shade on a branch of a kapok tree. It was brownish in colour, matching the tree branch. Then the chameleon crept into the sunlight onto a giant leaf and started to turn a bright green colour. Penny whispered in amazement, "Wow! That's what the teacher meant by camouflage. That was totally cool!"

Then the chameleon's body seemed to freeze, except for a round, bulgy eye on each side of its head. Both eyes kept rolling around in different directions, and Penny couldn't tell where the chameleon was looking. She wondered whether the animal stayed still because it knew it was being watched. Zap! The chameleon shot out its tongue and caught a cricket. "Eek!" squealed Penny.

That caused her to come out of her dream world, and she realized where she really was—the pet store. Penny moved on to the tarantula terrarium. It appeared to be empty. She peered cautiously through the glass and was careful not to tap on it because she thought the noise might scare the animal. Besides, she didn't want it to jump out and scare her! Penny spied the spider hiding under some leaves. She knew from watching a nature program that, for most people, a tarantula bite was no worse than a wasp sting. Still, the thought of a tarantula for a pet gave Penny the shivers!

Penny's attention was drawn next by the noisy chatter of the birds. They were dressed in all the colours of the rainbow. There were budgies, cockatiels, lovebirds, and even a blue and gold macaw parrot.

"I wonder if any of these birds can talk," Penny said to herself. Her curiosity was satisfied when the parrot suddenly squawked at her, "I can talk. Can you fly?"

Penny laughed. "No, but I wish I could!" she answered.

Penny found more fun at the fish tanks. She enjoyed making fish lips as she imagined talking to the fish in the aquariums. She discovered that tropical fish were different from goldfish. They needed a heater in their tank to keep the water warm. She thought the glassfish had a perfect name because she could see the bones of its skeleton!

Just then, Penny spotted a salesclerk taking a lizard-like creature out of a tank. "Whoa! What kind of animal is that?" asked Penny.

"This is a fire-belly newt," answered the salesclerk, as he showed her its bright orange tummy.

"That's another perfect name!" Penny blurted out. Even though the newt looked like a lizard, Penny knew from reading a library book that it was really an amphibian. This explained why its home was an aquarium with some water and a big rock.

After that, Penny wandered over to the glass cages where the guinea pigs, hamsters, mice, gerbils, and rats lived. She chuckled to herself when she saw a little hamster stuff an incredible amount of food into its cheeks. There was even a strange animal called a chinchilla that cleaned its fur by taking a dust bath. Another salesclerk explained to her that all these animals belonged to a special group of mammals called rodents. Penny was surprised to learn that rodents have four front teeth that never stop growing their whole lives. They keep these teeth worn down by chewing on things. She was disappointed to learn that most rodents do not live very long. One of the rats looked just like Ralph.

Penny had a big smile on her face when she got to cuddle a fluffy bunny rabbit. It was so cute, but large, and she laughed when she heard that its name was Baby.

𝒫enny's last stop was the puppies and kittens. She felt very lucky when she got there just in time to hold two friendly golden retriever puppies. Their names were Charlie and Molly, and they were from the same litter. That meant that they were brother and sister and were born at the same time. Most of the kittens were curled up in little balls, sound asleep. They all looked so sweet. Penny decided that her favourite was a black and white ball of fur that was yawning and stretching.

Penny's parents had been in the pet store the whole time and were watching her with interest. They were very proud of their daughter!

Chapter Four: Lucky Penny!

Then it was time to head home. Just as Penny walked into her house, the telephone rang. It was her Auntie Barb. The weather was sunny and warm, and she was inviting their family over for an afternoon swim and barbecue.

Penny's Auntie Barb and Uncle Steve and her cousins, Andrew and Sara, lived outside the city. Because it took about an hour to get there, Penny had plenty of time during the car ride to think about what she had seen and heard at the pet store.

By the time they arrived at her cousins' house, Penny knew for sure which kind of animal would be just right for her! She was now ready to pick her pet.

Andrew and Sara were waiting at the door with their two dogs, Roxie and Rex. Penny liked the way the dogs always licked her face and snuggled up next to her on the couch. They would do tricks—like sit, shake a paw, lie down, and roll over—and then wait for their treats.

Penny's Uncle Steve was always a lot of fun. While Auntie Barb barbecued the hamburgers and chicken, he played in the pool with Penny's dad and the cousins. Penny noticed that her mom was talking quietly to her aunt.

After dinner, everyone went into the family room where Penny, Andrew, and Sara had fun with Roxie and Rex and their dog toys.

The adults were smiling as they watched the children play with the dogs. Auntie Barb had the biggest smile of all.

"Penny, your mom was telling me before dinner how you have shown that you are responsible enough to have a pet of your own," said her aunt. "She also told me that you were at the pet store most of the morning, trying to figure out which kind of animal to choose for your pet. Have you come to a decision?"

"*Y*es. I've made up my mind. My two favourite animals are hamsters and dogs. I really enjoy my friend Emily's hamster, but I want a pet that will live a long time and be with me until I'm grown up," explained Penny. "It's so much fun playing with Roxie and Rex and taking my friend Jamie's two dogs for walks. I know a puppy would be the perfect pet for me!"

Auntie Barb laughed. "I'm glad to hear that because we have a surprise for you.

Do you remember the last time you were here, and we thought Roxie must be eating too much because she was getting chubby? Well, we found out that she's going to have babies, and you get to be the first to pick a puppy," her aunt announced.

Penny was thrilled! "Thank you! Thank you!" she shouted happily, jumping up and down and clapping her hands. Then she added, "It's so exciting! I'm finally going to have a pet!" Penny paused. "How long will it be before the puppies are born?"

Uncle Steve answered, "Roxie will have her babies in about a month, but you will have to wait longer to get your pet. The puppies will need to spend the first eight weeks of their lives with their mother and father and brothers and sisters. Then they will be old enough to be on their own."

Four weeks later, Roxie had her litter of five puppies. When Penny saw them, she fell in love with the littlest one. It had hair that was almost the same colour as hers.

Penny named her puppy PEANUT.

THE END

DEDICATED TO
MY MOTHER,
FLORENCE BROWN

–Mom, you have a "heart of gold"!
Thanks for always being there for me.

Text and illustrations copyright © 2007 Carol Szuminsky

Library and Archives Canada Cataloguing in Publication

Szuminsky, Carol, 1952-
Penny Picks the Perfect Pet / written by Carol Szuminsky
illustrated by Jenny Prest

ISBN-13: 978-0-9735579-1-6
ISBN-10: 0-9735579-1-5

1. Pets-Juvenile fiction. I. Prest, Jenny II. Title.

PS8637.Z85P45 2007   jC813'.6   C2007-900144-5

Illustration and Design by Jenny Prest

5 4 3 2 1 Printed in Canada by Printcrafters Inc.